Let's Trade

For Lynn Seiffer

PUFFIN BOOKS
Published by the Penguin Group
Penguin Books USA Inc., 375 Hudson Street, New York, New York 10014, U.S.A.
Penguin Books Ltd, 27 Wrights Lane, London W8 5TZ, England
Penguin Books Australia Ltd, Ringwood, Victoria, Australia
Penguin Books Canada Ltd, 10 Alcorn Avenue, Toronto, Ontario, Canada M4V 3B2
Penguin Books (N.Z.) Ltd, 182-190 Wairau Road, Auckland 10, New Zealand

Penguin Books Ltd, Registered Offices: Harmondsworth, Middlesex, England

First published in the United States of America by Puffin Books, 1989
Published simultaneously in Canada
Published in a Puffin Easy-to-Read edition, 1996

1 3 5 7 9 10 8 6 4 2

Text copyright © Harriet Ziefert, 1989
Illustrations copyright © Mary Morgan, 1989
All rights reserved

THE LIBRARY OF CONGRESS HAS CATALOGED THE PREVIOUS PUFFIN EDITION
UNDER THE CATALOG CARD NUMBER 88-62150
Puffin Books ISBN 0-14-050982-8

Puffin Easy-to-Read edition ISBN 0-14-038109-0

Puffin® and Easy-to-Read® are registered trademarks of Penguin Books USA Inc.
Printed in the United States of America

Reading Level 1.7

Let's Trade

Harriet Ziefert
Pictures by Mary Morgan

PUFFIN BOOKS

"Have a nice picnic!"
said Mom.

Meg, Sam, and Jo
took their lunch bags.

Then they went to the park.
Their cat went, too.

"I have a pickle and
grapes," said Meg.
"Sam, what do you have?"

"I have a banana,"
said Sam.
"And I'm sick of bananas!"

"I like bananas," said Meg.
"Let's trade."

Sam gave Meg the banana.
Meg gave Sam the pickle.

"What do you have?"
Meg asked Jo.

"I have peanut butter,"
said Jo.
"I'm sick of peanut butter!"

"I like peanut butter," said Meg.
"Let's trade."

Jo gave Meg the sandwich.
Meg gave Jo grapes.

"What do you have?"
Jo asked Meg.

"I have a banana and
I have peanut butter,"
said Meg.

"But you have *two* things!"
said Sam and Jo together.
"It's not fair!"

"I'll be fair!" said Meg.
"I'll share!"

Meg shared the banana.
Meg shared the sandwich.

"Now you have more than me!"
Meg said to Sam and Jo.
"You each have *three* things!"

Sam ate the pickle
and the peanut butter—
but *not* the banana!

"Remember," he said,
"I'm sick of bananas!"

Jo ate the grapes
and the banana—
but *not* the peanut butter.

"Remember," she said,
"I'm sick of peanut butter!"

Meg put her banana on top
of the peanut butter.
She ate it all up.
"Yummy!" she said.

"Yuck!" said Sam.
"Yuck!" said Jo.

"You wanted *my* food," said Meg.
"Now eat it all up!"

"I won't!" said Sam.
"I won't eat banana!"

"I won't," said Jo.
"I won't eat peanut butter."

"Just listen to me," said Meg.

"Sam, trade with Jo.
Jo, trade with Sam."

"You're bossy!" said Sam to Meg.
But he ate the peanut butter.

"You're mean!" said Jo to Meg.
But she ate the banana.

"Now let's play baseball,"
said Meg.

"I can't play," said Sam.
"My glove is too small."

"And I can't play," said Jo.
"My glove is too big."

Sam looked at Jo.
Jo looked at Sam.

"Let's trade!" said Sam.

"Okay! Play ball!"
said Meg.